GIRLS DON'T FARТ, Okay!!

Lisa Regan • Agnès Ernoult

Published by Bonney Press
an imprint of Hinkler Books Pty Ltd
45–55 Fairchild Street
Heatherton Victoria 3202 Australia
www.hinkler.com.au

Author: Lisa Regan
Illustrator: Agnès Ernoult
Prepress: Graphic Print Group

ISBN: 978 1 4889 0280 2

Printed and bound in China

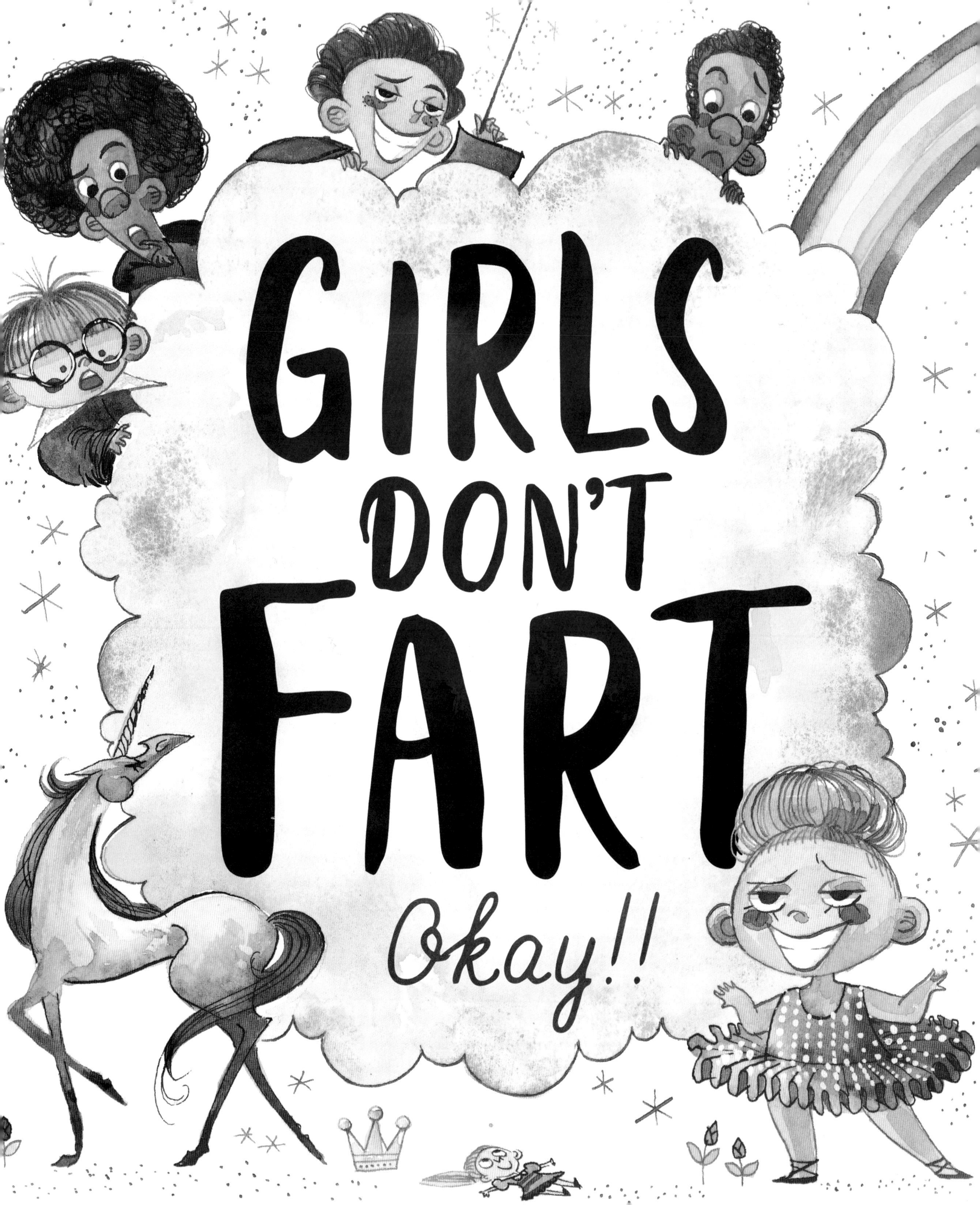
GIRLS DON'T FART
Okay!!

Ethan ate a lot of beans, which made his bottom rumble.

'Oh, Ethan! Stop that smell and noise!'

his family used to grumble.

But Ethan felt it wasn't fair.
He couldn't help his tummy.

He's surely not the only one whose toots upset his mummy.

So Ethan asked his group of friends,

'Does everyone get wind?'

Marty laughed,

Fizz looked confused

and Sam just quietly grinned.

But little Trixie took offence.

'Girls don't fart, okay!!

Only boys make bottom noise.

We girls aren't built that way.'

The boys just didn't believe her, so they set themselves a test.

To see if girls pass wind or not –

that would be their quest.

The school was serving eggs that day,
which made the boys all think.

'Now's our chance to check things out,
'cause this should raise a stink!'

They waited in the playground
where the girls all skip and jump.
And, listening very carefully, they heard a little '**flump**'.

'Aha!' they cheered,

'That's one confirmed! Let's try to find some more.'

Ethan waved his wand and they all vanished out the door.

They flew to the palace where they landed with a bump.

Bump!!

'No way!' they laughed. **'We'll never prove that royal females trump!'**

Princess Pearl played in her room, so to her door they went.

Thinking she was all alone, she let off a strawberry scent.

The boys crept
through the
bushes and past a
fancy fountain,

where they
gasped to see a
unicorn in the
shadow of
a mountain.

Ethan led them closer, and as the boys drew near,
all the colours of the rainbow erupted from her rear!

Their next stop was the ocean and
they dived beneath the waves.
Then Marty spied a pretty mermaid swimming in the caves.

The friends could hear the Mer-King, who was telling off his daughter,

he said it wasn't ladylike to make bubbles in the water.

Ethan cast
another spell
to whisk them
to a glade,

where Mrs Squirrel gathered nuts
while all her children played.

The boys watched oh-so-silently until they heard a flutter.

Mrs Squirrel did a fart that smelled of peanut butter!

'What a whiff!' the boys declared.

'Just wait 'til we tell Trixie!'

Then floating past their hiding place
flew a cheeky little pixie.

The boys crept along behind the pixie, following their noses.

Then spreading out behind her came pink clouds that smelled of roses.

Next, Ethan cast a spell that whisked them back to Marty's house.

They gathered in his bedroom, where they spied a lady mouse.

She ran behind the wardrobe and Fizz knelt to take a peek.

'Hee hee!' he laughed,

'The mouse just did a tiny bottom squeak!'

They heard a miaow and in a flash the mouse was on the run.

A kitten had started chasing her, trying to have some fun.

The kitten looked adorable, with soft white fluffy fur.

She was so relaxed that
she let out a stinky **'purrrrrr'**!

pooohhfftt

The boys had seen enough to prove to Trixie that she was wrong.
They were hurrying to find her when they heard a ballet song.

The ballerina did a fart. This was the best one yet!
Her smelly bottom made the dancer spin and pirouette!

Now they must find Trixie, to tell her what they'd seen.
They had enough proof to show that girls aren't always squeaky clea

Mermaids, dancers, lady mice, princesses as well –
making rainbows, bubbles, clouds of pink with
various sorts of smell.

Trixie and her friends were picking flowers in the park.

The sun was sinking in the sky and it was getting dark.

Suddenly they heard a noise – a gentle whispering sound.
Trixie flew up in the air, with glitter all around!

Trixie gasped and hid her face.
The fairies all went quiet.

'Caught in the act!' the boys all cried.
'Now you can't deny it!'